Book 1 in the Vantalos Family Adventure Series

The Magical Mystical Mirror

RJ Vantalos

Book design by FormattedBooks.com
Illustrations by Julia Geller

CHAPTER ONE

"Bryant. Tyler. Let's go. We're running late," Sienna yelled as she packed the Subaru Forester for the trip to Monterey. Sienna was always running late. As a single mom of two, time was never on her side. This weeklong vacation to Monterey would be a much-needed break from her job as Director of Worldwide Strategy at ProBio, a biotech firm headquartered in San Francisco.

"Hold on," Tyler said. Tyler was the youngest of the Vantalos children. At nine, she could read at the 7th-grade level and loved animals, especially marine animals. Part of the reason Sienna had decided to go to Monterey was so that Tyler could see the latest exhibits at the Monterey Bay Aquarium. She also found a great Airbnb, up in the hills of Carmel by the Sea called San Clemente Rancho. It was a bit far from where they normally stayed but she needed some nature time. The one thing she hoped for was clear skies. It had been raining for the past two weeks, uncommon for this time of year. If she could believe the forecasts, it was going to be clear skies for the entire week.

Clunk, clunk, clunk. Tyler was dragging a full-sized roller-type suitcase down the front narrow stairs of their Spanish-style house in the San Francisco Sunset neighborhood. It was filled with all her books, art supplies, spy gear, and stuffed animals.

"Tyler Mari Moraga Valdez Tico Vantalos! You cannot bring that suitcase with you. The car is packed! I already have your suitcase in here."

Tyler hated it when her mom used her full name. That usually meant she was annoyed with her.

"Mom. I need these things. We're gone for a week! What am I going to read?"

By this time, Bryant, the oldest at 12, strolled up playing Fortnite on his phone. Sienna had hesitated to buy him one but now that he was in middle school, it was impossible to hold off anymore. All his friends had one, and the last thing Sienna wanted was for Bryant to be different — he was already different enough.

Bryant was tall for his age. An avid reader like Tyler, he was mostly into sci-fi and comic books. He wanted to be a sci-fi writer and some of his short stories were published in the school newsletter — all of which were plastered on the Vantalos fridge along with Tyler's art and the family mantras, one of which is "Proceed as if Success is Inevitable."

"Ty. I told you Mom would not go for it." Bryant looked up from his phone as he walked over to help his mom finish packing.

"Shut up, Bry." Tyler was annoyed at her older brother. He knew how important her books were to her. Big brothers were always annoying.

"Bryant Julio Moraga Valdez Tico Vantalos. Help your sister take the suitcase back upstairs. We have to go. We're running late," Sienna said in a stern voice. Sometimes that was the only way to get her kids to get stuff done.

Both Tyler and Bryant knew that when their mom used their full names, she meant business. Sienna was always patient with her two children, or at least tried to be. She wanted them to know that she would be there for them, that they could count on her. Sometimes it was hard to be mom, dad, and the breadwinner, but she told herself that a one-parent household with stability and peace was better than a two-parent household with drama and discord.

Sienna was thankful for her job at ProBio. She had been there for over twenty years and had worked her way up from intern to Director of Worldwide Strategy. It was a stressful job, but it was also rewarding. Her boss Mark was always accommodating and since he was in Chicago, Sienna could work from home most days.

"Alright. Is everyone strapped in?" The car was finally loaded and Sienna had negotiated with Tyler for a much smaller backpack full of books, which was beside her in the back seat. Bryant was riding shotgun and in charge of music and navigation.

"Yup. All set," Tyler said as she looked up from her Boxcar Children book — she had read them all twice.

The drive from the Outer Sunset to Monterey takes about two hours, but that's without eating or bathroom breaks or the mandatory stop at the Dennis the Menace playground that even Bryant still liked.

"Mama, can we stop at the Dennis the Menace playground before we go to the beach?" Tyler said over the Kidz Bop CD that was playing over the stereo for what felt like the tenth time.

"Only for a little while since we need to get the cabin. It's far away from the beach." Sienna turned down the stereo as she ejected the CD and fumbled for anything other than Kidz Bop.

"Mom, how come we have to go there? It's boring. I want to go to the beach." Bryant had lifted his head from Toon Blast just enough to grimace at the thought of going to a playground.

"You used to love going. It will only be for a little while," Sienna said as she glanced over at Bryant, who was growing up too fast. Soon, he will be in high school and won't want to go on vacation with his little sister and mom, she thought.

The Dennis the Menace playground was just like Sienna remembered it. Tyler loved running over the bridge, and even Bryant was enjoying himself as he pretended to chase Tyler as a lava monster.

The ride from the playground to Carmel River Beach is a short one. Sienna had picked this beach because it was close to the road leading to San Clemente Rancho.

As they drove up, police, sheriff, and a park ranger, all with their lights flashing, blocked off the entrance to the parking lot.

"Ma'am. You need to turn around. The beach is closed today," the young deputy said as Sienna slowly pulled up to the parking lot.

"Why is it closed?" Sienna asked.

"The ranger found a bunch of sick sea otters. We're not sure why they are getting sick. As a precaution, we need to close the beach," the deputy said.

"Oh no. That's horrible," Tyler said out loud as she was stretching out of her car seat to hear what the deputy had to say. "The poor sea otters."

"Thank you, deputy. Do you know when it might be open?" Sienna asked as she told Tyler to sit back in her seat.

"Not sure, ma'am. Jim Golden, the biologist from Monterey Bay Aquarium, is down there now. It's up to them to tell us when it's safe."

"Okay." Sienna turned the car around and started to drive up Highway 1 to find the road to San Clemente Rancho.

"Mama, why are the sea otters sick?" Tyler asked with a concerned tone. She never liked to hear about or see sick animals.

"I don't know, honey. We can ask when we go to the aquarium tomorrow."

"Okay. Can we talk to the biologist?" Tyler loved talking to scientists. She loved the fact that they could answer all of her questions.

"We can ask, but he might be busy."

The drive to San Clemente Rancho took them east on Carmel Valley Road to the winding Robinson Canyon Road, which works its way through the beautiful Santa Lucia Preserve.

Cabin 84 is set back from the main road. It sits on stilts that make it look like a treehouse with a catwalk that goes to a loft mountain cabin, set back into a large oak tree.

"Mom, can I sleep in the Small Cabin? Please? Please? Please?" Tyler had jumped out of the car and run up the flight of stairs to the catwalk. She was running back and forth between the two — excited about the prospect of having her own house.

"We'll see. I need to unpack the car. Come down here and help Bryant and me." Sienna was tired from the drive and just wanted to settle in and enjoy the quiet.

The three-bedroom, two-bath Cabin 84 was a cozy place. It had been built in the '80s and the decorations seemed to be handmade with a lot of indigenous people artifacts and animal skulls. There were several books about the Rumsen, one of the eight groups of the Ohlone people who had made their home in the Carmel Valley.

"Mama, can you read us a story about the Rumsen before bed?" Tyler had been thumbing through the book The Rumsen of Carmel Valley. It was a tradition in the Vantalos household to read a story before bed. This had been something that Sienna's mom, Dori, had done when she was a kid. This reading before bed was one of the reasons both Tyler and Bryant loved to read. Sienna enjoyed this time as well. It was a great way to wind down the evening before bed.

"The Rumsen tribe held the lower Carmel River Valley and neighboring Monterey Peninsula at the time of Spanish colonization," Sienna started to read from the introduction. "Their population of approximately 400-500 people was distributed among at least five villages within their territory."

"What does territory mean?" Tyler asked since she loved to learn new words.

"That means where they lived. The Rumsen lived close to here. It also says that their spirit animal was the sea otter," Sienna answered.

Sienna finished the intro and then it was time to go to sleep. Tyler decided that sleeping in the small cabin was not a good idea. It was kinda creepy and she wanted to be close to her mom. Bryant felt the same way too.

As Tyler fell asleep, she wondered what was making the sea otters so sick. She was excited that tomorrow she might be able to ask someone.

CHAPTER TWO

Our Secret

The next day after a breakfast of pancakes and extra crispy bacon, they headed to the aquarium. Once they got their tickets, they headed straight to where the sea otters are kept. They were relieved to see a couple more sea otters than their last visit. Although, they could not be sure if they were the sick sea otters the deputy was talking about.

"I hope the extra sea otters we saw were the sick ones," said Tyler as they walked up to the sea otter holding area.

"It would take longer for a sea otter to recover, and when the ranger told us what happened, it sounded like it wouldn't be possible for them to recover that fast," Bryant said.

Sienna agreed.

By the time they had finished looking at the otters and two other exhibits, it was time for lunch and they were hungry!

After some pizza at Pizza Hut, they decided to split up. Sienna needed to find someone in charge of the otters.

"Bryant, take your sister to look around. Pay attention to your sister. Don't let her get lost. I am going to find someone who works here," said Sienna. Bryant groaned and groaned.

"Mom, how come I have to watch Tyler when you're not around to watch her? I always have to do that," Bryant whined.

"Bryant, we're all responsible for the people we love. Right now, you need to be responsible for your sister. Take Tyler to the gift shop and wait for me." Sienna was annoyed. Twelve-year-olds have so much drama.

"Alright. Let's go, Ty," squawked Bryant.

Bryant and Tyler trudged off to the gift shop while Sienna went to look for someone in charge of the sea otters.

"Bryant, Tyler, this is Dr. Golden. He is taking care of the sick sea otters," Sienna said as they found Tyler and Bryant looking at the calendars.

"Nice to meet both of you. Your mom tells me you wanted to know about the sick otters," Dr. Golden said in a smooth, kind voice.

Dr. Jim Golden was a big, strong man. He stood 6'1" and weighed over 200 pounds. Most of this weight came from working out by doing CrossFit and trudging around the ocean studying sea otters.

Dr. Golden was an expert in sea otters. He had fallen in love with marine biology at a young age. He was a rebellious kid who enlisted in the Navy at 18, became a Navy SEAL, and then went to school on the GI Bill. He then moved to Monterey and got his current job.

"If you want, I can take you to where we are keeping the sick otters. I was just about to go back when your mom approached me." Dr. Golden smiled at both of them and then at Sienna.

"Mom. Can we go? Please? Please?" Tyler was jumping up and down while raising her hand. Bryant looked bored as he rolled his eyes at all the excitement.

"If it's not too much trouble, Dr. Golden," Sienna said in her sweet voice, which was usually reserved for when Tyler or Bryant was upset.

"No trouble at all and, please, call me Jim." Jim smiled at Sienna and then back at Tyler and Bryant. "Okay, follow me!"

Tyler, Bryant, and Sienna followed Jim down to a "STAFF ONLY" entrance right next to the sea otter exhibit.

"Be careful. It's wet and slippery." Jim held the door open for all of them to follow him in.

The room smelled of seawater and fish with a hint of wet dirt. Jim led them past several cages where sick sea otters were staying.

"These are the otters that we saved from the mouth of the Carmel River. A lot of them are still sick. We're thankful we found them when we did." Jim was somber in his speech. You could tell that it made him upset that all the sea otters, ten total, were getting sick. It was clear he had no idea why.

"What are all these buckets?" Bryant pointed to a set of buckets stacked up, one on top of the other, like a pyramid. In black Sharpie, each bucket had a code on it, CRS-001 to CRS-015, as well as a biohazard sticker on the lid.

"Those are soil samples from around the mouth of the Carmel River. We suspect that whatever is making the otters sick is somehow coming from there. Make sure not to touch them. We're not sure what could be in it." Jim had some concern in his voice.

At that moment, Jim's cellphone rang. He looked at the number and said, "Excuse me. This is an important call I must take. Feel free to look around, but please don't touch anything." Jim promptly left through another door as he answered his phone.

"It's so sad that they are all sick," Tyler said, looking at the cages of the sea otters, stacked on stilts, three cages high. The bottom cage was as tall as she was.

"I know. I'm glad they are here and not somewhere else. They must be scared." Sienna was looking into one of the cages with the name tag "Buddy" written on it in black Sharpie.

Bryant had walked towards the back of the room. There was a single cage tucked away in the back with one of the buckets on a stand, next to the cage. The label was CRS-016 and the top of the lid was off. The top of the bucket came to about Bryant's waist. The nametag on the cage said "River."

"Hi, River. I'm Bryant," Bryant spoke softly to the sick sea otter. As he leaned down to speak to River, he put his hand on the outside of the oxidized cage.

"Ouch!" Bryant screamed. His finger got cut on the edge of River's cage. "That hurt."

"Bryant. What happened?" Sienna heard Bryant's scream. Sienna and Tyler hurried over to see what had happened.

"I cut myself on River's cage. See." Bryant held up his finger. It was a deep scratch with blood dripping down his finger. "It hurts. What should I do?"

"Hold it away from you. I have a sanitized wipe in my purse. We need to clean it so that it doesn't get infected." Sienna's voice was half concerned and half annoyed that Bryant touched something that he shouldn't have.

"Mom, it hurts," Bryant moaned and started to shake his finger to try and made the pain go away. As he shook his hand, the blood from his finger splattered into the open bucket.

"I hope you are okay," a low voice said.

"Who said that?" Sienna was startled by the new voice in the room.

"Don't be afraid," the voice said again.

"Really! This is silly. Who's there?" Sienna gathered up Tyler and Bryant behind her with their backs to the wall, facing River's cage.

"Down here," the voice said again. Sienna, Bryant, and Tyler looked down at River. "It's me. River. I hope you're going to be okay."

Sienna, Bryant, and Tyler could not believe what they were hearing.

"You can talk!" Sienna said in a high-pitched voice, startled that a sea otter could talk. "How can that be?"

"I don't know. I thought I could always talk. I'm shocked you can hear me," River said. After River said "me," her speech turned to high-pitched barks.

"What happened? Why can't you talk anymore?" Sienna asked.

"Bark, bark, bark," River said.

"This is so odd. What did you do?" Sienna looked at Bryant, who was as shocked as she was. Tyler's jaw was still open. If it were open any wider, it would have hit the floor.

Just then, Jim came back into the room.

"Sorry about that. They found some more sick otters and I have to go look at them. Oh. What happened to your finger, Bryant? Let me clean that for you so it doesn't get infected." Jim took the first aid kit off the wall and opened it up. He proceeded to clean and bandage Bryant's finger.

"There you go. Good as new. Sorry about this, but I have to get going and you can't stay here. I'll escort you out." Jim put the first aid kit back on the wall and walked to the staff door they had come in. "Well. C'mon. There are sick otters to attend to," Jim said as Sienna, Bryant, and Tyler were looking at Jim and then River and then back at Jim. Sienna broke the silence.

"Okay... Come on, kids. Let's get going. Jim has work to do." Sienna smiled at Jim as they filed out. Jim closed and locked the door behind him.

"Why don't you guys come back tomorrow, and I can finish the tour." Jim was smiling at Sienna, hoping she would say yes to come again.

"Um. Sure. We can come back. What time?"

"How about lunch? My treat for having to cut things short today."

"Um. Sure. That works."

"Great. See you tomorrow." With that, Jim walked out a side door. Sienna, Bryant, and Tyler looked at each other and headed to the car.

CHAPTER THREE

NEW LAND, NEW FRIENDS

"**M**om, how come we could hear River? Are we special? Is he special? OMG! OMG! OMG! What are we going to do? How come you didn't tell Jim?" Tyler was rattling off so many questions it was making Sienna's head spin.

"Slow down. Let me think. Remember what I always say." Sienna was trying to make sense of it all as well. How could a sea otter talk? It just made no sense.

"Yeah. Yeah. Drama free; way to be. Blah, Blah. Geez, Mom. If there is one thing we can have drama over, it's a talking sea otter!" Tyler was in rare form. She was easily excited but was also good at stating the obvious.

"I'm not sure why we could hear him. Let's get to the car and get back to the cabin. It's getting late." Sienna had no idea what to think of all this. Bryant had been the closest to River when he started to talk. Maybe he touched something.

The ride back to Cabin 84 was quiet. Sienna put on Tracy Chapman to calm her nerves. Tyler was reading in the back while Bryant was playing Toon Blast again. Sienna would usually tell him to stop, but she was too deep in thought to notice.

"Kids. Make sure to grab all our stuff, especially the books." Sienna had just pulled up in front of the cabin and was talking over her shoulder as she stepped out of the car to gather up the snacks and books. Tyler ran up the steps and turned the doorknob over and over again.

"C'mon, Mom. Hurry up. I want to read about the Rumsen. I bet there is something in that book about magical sea otters."

"Stop doing that, Tyler. You're going to break the door-knob." Sienna made it to the top of the stairs and slid the key in the lock. Tyler quickly turned in and ran into the room. He headed straight for the book on the Rumsen.

Tyler thumbed through the book and, after a couple of minutes, she held up the book and pointed to one of the paragraphs.

"I knew it. See. It says right here." Tyler was excited like she had found buried treasure or the secrets to the universe or where her mom hid her birthday presents. "It says that the Rumsen thought that the sea otters were magical. Mom, can you read it?" Tyler ran over to Sienna, who was unpacking the groceries they had bought before coming back.

"Where does it say that?" Sienna grabbed the book and put on her reading glasses.

"Right there. Second paragraph. See, it says 'magical'." Tyler's eyes were as big as a cat focusing on one of those feather stick toys. Bryant walked over to look as well. He looked annoyed.

"No, it doesn't. How can sea otters be magical?"

"Bryant, don't be mean to your sister." Sienna pulled the book closer and started to read out loud.

"The Rumsen believed that their ancestors came back to them as sea otters. The sea otter, or Nee'gig, is different from the normal land otter, or Keoonik, which is translated as 'trickster.' The Rumsen hunted normal otters for their pelts while the sea otters were never hunted.

The Rumsen would visit the sea often and bring offerings to the sea otters as a tribute to their ancestors. Some Rumsen legends talk about a magical plate that the medicine man would use to communicate to the sea otters. Legend has it that the sea otters would tell the medicine man about how good the harvest would be or when it was safe to drink the water in the stream, which is now called the Carmel River."

"Hmmm. That's interesting. You're right, Tyler. It says something about a magical plate but not that the sea otters are magical." Sienna closed the book and took off her reading glasses to massage the bridge of her nose. She often did this when she was trying to figure out a tough problem at work or how she was going to fit all the chores, grocery shopping, and kid chauffeuring into a day.

"See, Bry. I told you. There is something magical about the Rumsen and sea otters. I just know it." Tyler had a satisfied smile on her face, like how she envisioned Encyclopedia Brown's face when he solved a case.

"It still does not mean they are magical. We don't even know how we could hear River," Bryant said matter-of-factly as he looked at the bandaged cut on his index finger.

"All I know is that all of us heard River speak. Either all of us are crazy or we did something when we were at the aquarium. Bryant, did you touch anything when you were near River?" Sienna asked just like Encyclopedia Brown would. Tyler would know since she had read them all.

"I don't think so. I leaned down, put my hand on the cage, it got cut, and then we heard River speak." Bryant was counting on his fingers the steps as he spoke them. Tyler interrupted his concentration.

"Mom, maybe there are more books about the Rumsen in the small cabin outback. When I went in yesterday, I saw a bunch of antiques and books. Maybe there are some more clues there."

"Good idea, Tyler. C'mon, guys, let's go." Sienna picked up the Rumsen book and headed to the door. Bryant and Tyler followed her across the bridge to the cabin. Sienna opened the door and turned on the light to reveal a room with an antique bed and dresser. A ratty, lime-green easy chair was in the corner next to a floor-to-ceiling faded brown bookshelf, packed with old books. Next to the bookshelf, hanging on the wall, was an old, cloudy mirror that had seen better days.

"Look, Mom. Another book on the Rumsen! This one looks a lot older." Bryant was at the bookshelf, pulling out the books one at a time. "It looks like it's in a different language." Bryant leaned on the wall next to the mirror. His cut hand slipped, bumped the mirror, and the blood from his cut finger smeared across the mirror. "Oh no," Bryant said. "I'm sorry, Mom, I slipped."

Just as Bryant said, 'I slipped,' there were bright lights and loud noises, like air whooshing by at supersonic speed. When the sound stopped, the light turned back to normal, but what they saw was anything but normal.

"Mom, why are we dressed like olden people?" Tyler was looking down at her clothes, which looked like the ones she had seen in her history books about when the Spanish first came to California with the Juan Bautista de Anza expedition.

Sienna looked down at her clothes as well. "I don't know. Where are we?"

As they got the focus back in their eyes from the bright light, the place they found themselves in was a picture right out of Tyler's Juan Bautista de Anza expedition history book. As the three of them looked around, there was something else that was off.

"Tyler, I can tell it's your voice, but you don't look like you." Sienna was looking at what she thought was Tyler, given the voice. What she saw was a girl of similar age but with more pronounced Spanish features — like the old pictures her mom would show her about their family back in the late 1700s.

"What do you mean, Mom? Mom! Is that you? You don't look like you either." Tyler was experiencing the same thing. The woman in front of her looked vaguely like her mom. They both looked over at Bryant.

"Bryant, you don't look like you either," Sienna said as she looked at both of them and then around, to figure out what had just happened.

The place where they were now looked like the courtyard at Mission San Carlos Borromeo de Carmelo that they had visited before. Tyler had written a report on it because one of her distant relatives, Sergeant Antonio Dela Moraga Tico, had passed through on his way to the San Francisco Presidio. Antonio's sister, Olivia, had come over from Spain with her two kids, Juana and Jose, to seek a better life. No one knew what happened to Olivia's husband, Ernesto.

"Buenos dias, Señorita Tico. Hola, Juana and Jose." A man walked by and tipped his hat to Señorita Tico (Sienna) and waved to Juana (Tyler) and Jose (Bryant).

"Buenos dias," Sienna said with a smile, trying to figure out how she could speak Spanish.

"Mom, you can speak Spanish!" Bryant said with shock. "What's going on?"

Sienna was thinking the same thing.

As Sienna was deciding what they should do next, a bright light blinded her with the same supersonic air whooshing as before. When the light returned to normal, they were back in the small cabin.

"MOM. WHAT HAPPENED?" Tyler was wide-eyed, talking slowly and deliberately. It took Sienna a couple of seconds to react.

"We must have activated a time portal. I only thought stuff like that was science fiction." Sienna looked at Bryant and Tyler. One, to make sure they were safe and two, to make sure they looked like Bryant and Tyler. "There is something about this room that's magical."

Sienna started to look around when she saw the smudge of Bryant's blood on the old mirror. It was no longer red but glowing. Actually, it was flickering, like a candle.

"How come my blood is flashing like that?" Bryant asked as they all moved in for a closer inspection.

Sure enough, the smudge of blood that Bryant put on the old mirror was flickering and then, all of a sudden, it disappeared.

"Did you see that?" Tyler asked in an excited voice. "It vanished!"

"That it did. So strange." Sienna was massaging the bridge of her nose. This was a perplexing development.

"Mom, I'm starving." Bryant grabbed his stomach.

"So am I." Tyler did the same movement as Bryant.

"Yeah, I'm starving too. Let's go back to the main house and eat. I need to think more about this."

Sienna followed Bryant and Tyler out of the small cabin to the main cabin. As she was about to turn the light off, she looked back at the old mirror — it looked just like it had when they first came in.

CHAPTER FOUR

UNLIKELY FRIENDS

D r. Golden picked Crystal Fish on Lighthouse Avenue for lunch since it had great food and easy parking. He had texted Sienna the address after dinner and promptly met them at 11:30 a.m. when they opened for lunch.

"Dr. Golden. Nice to see you again," Sienna said as they walked up, their usual twenty minutes late. "Sorry, we're late."

"No problem and, please, call me Jim. Do you guys like Japanese?" Jim asked, looking at Tyler and Bryant.

"Yes. I love it. I love Vegetable Tempura and Agedashi Tofu," Tyler spouted off. "Bryant's not as big a fan, but Mom always says he needs to eat more than just burgers and fries."

"Ty, you know I eat more than that." Bryant looked up from his phone.

"Tyler and Bryant. Please. We're about to eat." Sienna blushed a little bit, hoping that Bryant and Tyler would behave.

"Well, I'm sure we can find something for everyone to eat here," Jim said, smiling at Sienna as they were taken to their table.

"Do you know what's making the sea otter's sick yet?" Tyler asked the first question before they had even sat down.

"No, not yet. It's perplexing. The symptoms are nothing like we have seen before. The police think that it's industrial waste from the biotech companies upstream from Carmel River Beach. The companies deny it, of course. The Feds are coming out as well since the sea otters are an endangered species. That means they are protected and it's a federal crime to hurt them."

"How awful. I hope it's not industrial waste. Do you know the names of the companies they suspect?" Sienna asked as the food arrived.

"Not offhand, but I can get that to you."

"Please do. I work for ProBio up in San Francisco and we might be able to help."

"That would be great. We need all the help we can get." Jim smiled at Sienna and she smiled back.

After lunch, which Jim insisted he pay for over Sienna's objections, they walked down Lighthouse Avenue towards the aquarium.

"Mom. Can we go into BookBuyers? Please, please, please?" Tyler was jumping up and down as they passed the bookstore, which sold all sorts of used books.

"Not right now, Tyler. We need to get to the aquarium. Maybe when we come back," Sienna said calmly.

Tyler wanted to go to a bookstore, but Sienna wanted to get to the aquarium to hunt for more clues. In fact, she wanted to go as well to find the book The Mystical Adventures of Juan Bautista de Anza in the Carmel Valley that had been referenced multiple times in The Rumsen of Carmel Valley book she read last night after their trip back in time.

The book had a series of paintings in it. One was a woman with two kids and the other was a Native American medicine man. The captions said:

Olivia Maria Moraga Tico with her son Jose and daughter Juana circa 1800 at Mission Carmel.

Rumsen Medicine Man Speaks with Otters at Mission Carmel circa 1800.

The black and white paintings looked a lot like the people they had become when transported back in time. When Sienna did more research, she found that Olivia was the sister of Sergeant Antonio De la Tico, who had come over from the Catalonia region of Spain.

The Mystical Adventures of Juan Bautista de Anza in the Carmel Valley was written by Ernesto de la Cruz in the 1900s and had been translated from Spanish in the 1950s.

A quick Internet search found that it had been out of print for over 100 years. No luck on Amazon either.

The particular section that had the picture of Olivia was about the rituals the Rumsen medicine man taught the de Anza expedition. In particular, Olivia had learned a little Rumsen, which made it easier for her to learn how the Rumsen did their rituals.

All of the reading and research Sienna did made it clearer and clearer that there was a connection between her family and why they went to the past. It was just too much of a coincidence that her, Tyler, and Bryant could hear River and travel back to Carmel in the late 1700s.

As they continued to walk along Lighthouse Avenue, Jim started to talk about what they were going to see once they got to the aquarium.

"Last night, we got a couple more otters that were sick. We're going to go back and see them, along with where we do a lot of our research."

They cut down a side street to Cannery Row, walking past Highway 1 Gold, Games & Grub, Mrs. Laurie's Palm & Tarot Reader, and Lilly Mae's Baked Goods, with the smell of freshly baked cinnamon rolls floating down the street.

Jim led them around the side, past the Members Entrance, and into the employee side entrance with a swipe of his ID badge.

"Be careful. It's slippery," Jim said as he held the door open for them all.

Once inside, they could smell the salt water and mix of rotting fish and bleach. Jim opened another door and they were now near the tank that held the sharks.

"Watch your head. It's a bit tight. We had to move the otters to a place with more room. Usually, this area is for the sharks and kelp forest, but we have so many sick otters, we ran out of room."

As they ducked their heads and walked down the narrow hallway, Jim came to a hatch and spun the handle around to open it up.

"The only place we could put them is in the isolation room. That's why the big hatch. Once you get in, you might feel some pressure or a whooshing sound. That's the negative pressure to keep anything bad in. Once I close the hatch, it should feel normal."

When Jim opened the hatch, they heard the whooshing sound and, as promised, the pressure equalized when he closed and spun the hatch closed.

"Alright, here is where we keep all the otters we find that are sick." Jim was standing to the side of the hatch, and behind him was a row of pens and a massive tank down the middle. Each pen had a sliding gate that gave access to the tank. There must have been ten per side. "We have to isolate them so they don't get each other sick, but we also have to give them access to water," Jim said as he swept his hand around in the air.

Stacked behind Jim were the same orange buckets with the biohazard stickers and the same number scheme. The number of buckets matched the number of otters.

The tour lasted about an hour, with Jim doing most of the talking. It was clear that whatever was making the sea otters sick needed to be found soon. The aquarium was running out of room to house them, and releasing the healthy sea otters would do no good. They had done that the week before. River had been released and she had come back even sicker.

After the tour, Jim let them out through the side entrance. Sienna and Jim had made plans to have dinner later at Spinnaker to catch up since Sienna had promised to do some research on the biotech companies that were upstream from Carmel River Beach. Thankfully, there were only a few companies to research.

The walk back along Cannery Row was filled with tourists, sometimes six deep. This annoyed Tyler, who wanted to get off the main street and back up to Lighthouse so they could go to BookBuyers.

As they weaved their way in between the tourists, they bumped into a table that was crammed along the sidewalk.

"Sorry. It's so crowded that it's hard to navigate," Sienna said as she turned around to see who she had bumped into and where Tyler and Bryant were.

"It's okay, Olivia," a raspy voice said under a wide-brimmed sun hat, right outside Mrs. Laurie's Palm & Tarot Reader.

"Olivia! Why did you call me Olivia?" Sienna stopped in her tracks, her eyes wide and searching for who the voice was under the hat.

Slowly, the sun hat tipped up to reveal a woman's face. Oldish, but not wrinkly — probably because she wore a sun hat on days like today.

"Oh. Sorry. I sensed you were someone else," Mrs. Laurie of Mrs. Laurie's Palm & Tarot Reader said in a soft voice. "Honest mistake." She put her head back down and went back to reading her book.

Sienna was not into all the woo woo of palm readers or the like. She did have crystals, but more because she liked the way they looked and not for their 'aura-cleansing properties.' She did try to buy organic since all the pesticides and Genetically Modified Organisms (GMOs) made her nervous. She had good reason to be. The scientists she worked with at ProBio were always overly optimistic about a finding. She was used to making certain assumptions about their 'breakthroughs.' That's the reason her iPhone was 4 generations behind, and she yearned for the days of her old Nokia that could actually make a decent call.

"Whoa. Mom. She called you Olivia," Tyler said as they both looked at the sun hat.

"Excuse me. Mrs. Laurie. How much for a reading?" Sienna did not know why those words had come out of her mouth, but they had.

Mrs. Laurie put her book down and slowly tilted up her head and smiled. "For old friends, the first one is free."

"Old friends? What do you mean by old friends?" Sienna was perplexed and a bit confused. This whole trip was getting weirder and weirder.

"Come on in and let's get started." Mrs. Laurie waved them in and they filed into Mrs. Laurie's Palm & Tarot Reader, which was a converted dentist's office. At least that's what it looked like.

"Now. What should I call you?"

"Sienna. My name is Sienna."

"Sienna. Yes. What would you like to know?"

"Umm. Well, for starters, why did you call me Olivia and say that we are old friends?"

"Because we are. Well, at least in a past life. We have met before...a long time ago. Your name was Olivia then."

"How do you know that?"

"I don't know. I just know. It's a gift."

"I have a question." Tyler raised her hand like she was in class.

"Tyler. Please. Don't interrupt," Sienna said.

"It's no trouble, Juana. What's your question?"

"Juana? My name is Tyler," Tyler said with a pout on her face.

"Yes. Indeed it is. I'm sorry. What's your question?"

"How come we can talk to sea otters and go back in time?"

"Well, Tyler, those are two questions." Mrs. Laurie smiled and picked up the book she was reading. "Look familiar?"

Mrs. Laurie turned the book around to reveal the title:

The Mystical Adventures of Juan Bautista de Anza in the Carmel Valley

"MOM! That's the book! That's the book!" Tyler reached for the book, but Sienna grabbed her hand before she should reach it.

"Tyler. That's not polite. It's not ours." It was always a struggle to keep Tyler in line. She always got so excited.

"It's okay. Here you go." Mrs. Laurie handed the book to Tyler. She thumbed through it.

"Wow. This is awesome. It's so old."

"Yes, it is. It's an old book full of old stories about the Rumsen and Juan Bautista de Anza. The answers to your questions are in here, Sienna. Why don't you borrow it for a while? Bring it back when you're done."

"That's generous of you, but we can't," Sienna said as she took the book from Tyler and gave it back to Mrs. Laurie.

"Sienna, we are old friends. I trust you with it. Please. Read it. Find what you are looking for."

CHAPTER FIVE

HISTORY COMES TO LIFE

S ienna thought it best to stay in town since it would be forty-five minutes each way back to the cabin.

The 'talk' with Mrs. Laurie had generated more questions than answers. She could not believe that Mrs. Laurie had called her Olivia and that she had the book she was looking for. It was all so strange, yet she knew that some of the answers to her questions would be in the book.

Sienna decided to take Tyler and Bryant to the public library on Pacific so that she could read the book. Libraries were a big part of their lives. Both Tyler and Bryant read a lot of books. Sienna always felt that physical books were the best way to learn. There was something about the feel of a book that made you more engaged.

The Mystical Adventures of Juan Bautista de Anza in the Carmel Valley was old and worn. The pages were thick and had a brownish tint like someone had spilled coffee on them. Thankfully, this copy was in English.

As she opened the front cover, there was an inscription on the inside flap that read:

To Laurie. I value your friendship so much. All my love, Olivia.

"This gets weirder and weirder," Sienna whispered to herself as she flipped to Chapter 1, after skimming the introduction and the translator's notes.

Chapter 1: Juan Bautista de Anza meets the Rumsen

Sienna sat back and adjusted her reading glasses to get the olden type in better focus and started to read.

"The Rumsen came out of the Carmel Valley to meet the Bautista expedition. The soldiers of the expedition, led by Sergeant Tico, had their weapons drawn while the Rumsen, shorter than the Spanish and dressed in furs, walked right up to Bautista, and started to point to Mrs. Olivia Tico.

Since neither spoke each other's language, Bautista sent for a translator from Mission Carmel. Once the translator came, the conversation centered around the sacred grounds that they were on. It was revealed that the Rumsen's medicine man, Speaks with Otters, had foretold their arrival."

Sienna read on as the chapter detailed the first meeting of Bautista and the Rumsen. The gist of it was that the Rumsen felt that the Spanish were their lost ancestors and that Olivia Tico was a special person that they needed to pass on the magic to so she could speak with sea otters.

Chapters 2 through 5 were more of the same. They detailed the interactions with Bautista and the Rumsen, as well as mentioned several times that Olivia was learning from Speaks with Otters the ancient ways of the Rumsen.

It was not until Chapter 6, The Magic Shinny, that the details of this training came to light in this paragraph.

"It was revealed to Olivia that there is a special cave that contains the magic shinny. This substance holds the secret to speaking with the sea otters. The Rumsen have fashioned a plate out of the material."

The rest of the chapter talked about the details of the rituals but nothing about how the plate was used. For whatever reason, it was left out.

As Sienna flipped to the last chapter, she noticed several pictures. These were the same pictures as in the other book.

"Strange," Sienna said softly to herself. "These look like the same pictures, but the one of Olivia looks different." As Sienna brought the picture close to her, she noticed something around Olivia's neck that was not in the other picture. "What is that?" Sienna said as she took her glasses off to get a better look. "It looks like an hourglass or something. I wonder why it's not in the other picture."

Just as she put the book down, Tyler and Bryant came over to the table. "Mom, I'm hungry. Can we get a snack or something?" Bryant said in his usual way. He was always hungry. Sienna wondered where all the food went since he was rail thin.

"Yeah. We can go in a minute," Sienna said as she looked between the two books. "Can you look at this and tell me what you see?" she said to Bryant, hoping that his young eyes would see more than she could.

"What am I looking for?" Bryant asked as he picked up the book.

"What's around Olivia's neck? I can't seem to make it out."

"It's an hourglass. A small hourglass." Bryant handed back the book to his mom.

"That's what I thought. Thanks. Yes. We can go get a snack. Let's go down to Cannery Row and walk around."

"Can we go to Lilly Mae's and get a cinnamon roll? I love those. It makes my tummy smile," Bryant said with wide eyes.

"Gross. They are sooo chewy. Let's get cookies at Nestlé Toll House. Those are much better," Tyler said, jumping around.

"Tyler, don't yunk your brother's yum. We can go to both places but first, we need to get some protein. All that sugar is going to make you sick."

Sienna had carefully bookmarked a bunch of pages to read in The Mystical Adventures of Juan Bautista de Anza in the Carmel Valley. Over a falafel plate at Paprika Cafe, Sienna thumbed through her bookmarked pages, trying to find anything she might have missed.

As she skimmed Chapter 4, Interactions with the Rumsen, she noticed the word 'hourglass' for the first time.

"Interesting. It says here that the Rumsen made hourglasses as a way to 'be in time with nature.' At least that's the way it's translated," Sienna mumbled as Tyler and Bryant looked on, mouths full of falafel.

The rest of the bookmarked chapters yielded little to nothing that she didn't already know. It was clear from her research that Olivia learned some of the Rumsen traditions, but the details of them were spotty.

One chapter did talk about the magic plate, while the other dismissed it as only a way to reflect the sun. Apparently, the reflection of the sun on the plate is what attracted the sea otters to come closer.

The rest of the afternoon was spent walking Cannery Row and, as promised, going to Lilly Mae's and Nestlé Toll House for a snack.

Dinner with Jim was lovely. He had been busy all day at Carmel River Beach with more sick sea otters. He said again that if they didn't find a solution soon, they were going to have to ship the otters off. That was not ideal since the only other place to keep them was the Marine Mammal Center up north. It also had limited capacity.

"It's a real mystery," Jim said as he dug into his crème brûlée. "It looks like the otters are being poisoned, but it's hard to tell by what. The biotech company upstream is still adamant that it's not them, but I'm skeptical. I have never seen anything like this before. It's got to be them. What else can it be?"

"It sure seems that way. I was going to check with some people at ProBio about it. Sorry. I have not done that yet. I have been reading about the Rumsen and de Anza. Do you know about them?" Sienna said after she spooned up some more of her crème brûlée.

"Oh. The Rumsen. Yes. I have heard of them. We sometimes find artifacts along the Carmel River. I have a bunch back at the office. If you're interested, I can show you tomorrow." Jim smiled as he ate the last of his crème brûlée.

Sienna smiled back. "That would make three days in a row that we saw each other. Are you sure it's no trouble?"

"Not at all. Not at all." Jim smiled back.

"Well, if it's no trouble then, sure, we'll come by tomorrow."

They set up a time late in the morning to meet in Jim's office. After an after-dinner espresso and cappuccino, they bid farewell, and Sienna, Tyler, and Bryant made the trek back to Cabin 84.

As Sienna drove the winding road back, she could not get two things out of her mind: 1) how Olivia learned the traditions of the Rumsen and 2) how the hourglass fit into all this.

Back at the cabin, Sienna settled in to read more of both books. She knew that the answer had to be somewhere in these two volumes. The question was where...

As she skimmed past the bookmarked pages, she came upon a paragraph she did not remember reading.

"Rumsen medicine men carry an hourglass around their neck. Legend has it that the hourglass is meant to tell them when the sea otters will return to the sea. Without the hourglass, the ritual of the calling cannot be performed."

The calling? What could that be?

As she took off her glasses and massaged the bridge of her nose, she decided to take a walk outside to clear her head. As she walked out the front door, she looked over at the small cabin. The door was ajar. Curious, she went over to close it but instead, she walked in and turned on the light.

The room was exactly like they had left it the day before. The glow of Bryant's blood was gone but she noticed something else, hanging from the left side of the mirror.

"What is that?" Sienna said softly to herself as she walked closer.

As she moved in, the object came into focus.

It was an hourglass on a leather chain. Sienna walked closer, took it off the mirror, and looked at it. It glistened in the light — just like when Bryant had spilled his blood on the mirror.

As she looked at the hourglass some more, she turned it upside down.

Whoosh!

A bright light engulfed Sienna, and when she could focus, she was back in the place they were before, but this time, she had the hourglass with her.

"Buenos dias, Señorita Tico." A man walked by, same as before.

Sienna looked around and saw Jose and Juana. This time, they spoke Spanish, but she could understand it.

Sienna looked down at the hourglass and turned it back the other way. At first, nothing happened. She waited and then...

Whoosh!

She was back in the small cabin.

She tipped the hourglass a couple more times and the same thing happened. It was all starting to make sense.

The hourglass is what triggers the transport, at least one of the ways. Once it runs out, you come back to the present world.

To test this out, she went outside with just the hourglass. She tipped it over and nothing happened.

"It must be that you have to be close to the mirror for this to work," Sienna mumbled to herself.

"Tyler, Bryant. Look what I found." Sienna had closed the small cabin door and gone back to the big cabin. "It's the hourglass in the picture."

Sienna then explained to them what she had learned and how maybe by using the mirror and the hourglass they could figure out what was making the sea otters sick.

CHAPTER SIX

SPEAKS WITH OTTERS

"Okay. So do you guys understand the plan?" Sienna had spent the better part of an hour going over how they were going to help the sea otters.

Sienna had spent more time going back and forth to the past. She tried to take various things with her and quickly realized that the only thing that came with her was the hourglass. She also figured out that the hourglass had about two hours of time to elapse. She also confirmed that every

time she went back, she went to the exact same place —
Mission Carmel.

"Yes. I think so," Tyler said while Bryant nodded his head.
The 'plan' was simple.

Sienna, Bryant, and Tyler would all go back together.
Sienna had thought about not bringing them but quickly
realized she needed as many brains as possible to remember
the details. She had placed a notebook on the dresser, next
to the mirror, along with a bunch of pens. This was to record
as many details as possible from each trip.

In terms of exploration, Sienna had determined that
the four corners of the mission faced roughly north, south,
east, and west with a high mound towards the north. For the
first four trips, at least, they would make sure they walked
from each corner.

"We need to stick together," Sienna said. "Make sure that
you see me at all times. We'll start with a short trip. Ready?"

"Ready," Tyler and Bryant said almost at the same time.
Whoosh!

"Buenos dias, Señorita Tico." It was the same man they
had seen before. Sienna (Olivia) looked at Tyler (Juana)
and Bryant (Jose) and nodded.

"You guys ready to go?" Sienna said. In her mind, it
was English. When it came out, it was Spanish. Juana and
Jose nodded.

Mission Carmel, or rather Mission San Carlos Borromeo
del Río Carmelo, was founded on August 1st, 1771 after being
moved from its original location in Monterey by Junípero
Serra. It was the second mission built by Franciscan

missionaries in Alta California. From what Sienna could gather, it was somewhere in the late 1700s. She based that on the pictures she had seen in the various books she had read. The first order of business was to figure out the date.

"As we walk around, look for anything with a date," Sienna said as they set off, roughly going north. As they walked, there was not much — some random huts and a well. Sienna looked at the hourglass and noticed that it was still three-quarters full.

"Mom, there is not much out this way and we're about to hit a bunch of trees," Bryant said since he was a little ahead of Sienna and Tyler.

"Yes. It looks that way. Just a lot of woods and that big hill." Sienna was walking slowly as she looked around. "Let's head back to the mission."

They turned around and walked back to the courtyard of the mission, where friars and native people were busy working on sorting grain and tending livestock. The native people did not look happy.

"Mom, the natives look so sad. Why is that?" Tyler said as they walked by a group of natives sorting grain.

"I'm not sure. Let's try and find the mission office. Maybe they have a book or something that tells the date," Sienna said as they walked past baskets of grain.

They walked east, which seemed to be where some newer builds were just being finished. The new buildings were directly opposite the main building, which had a cross on it. As they approached the newer building, Sienna noticed a native man in a bear head with an hourglass around his neck.

As she passed by, the man said something in a language she did not understand. The only thing she understood was her name.

"Mom, I think that's Speaks with Otters. What did he say?" Bryant said.

"I don't know. I could only make out my name." Sienna smiled back at the man as they walked past. The man turned around and said something else, and Sienna turned around, smiled back, and nodded.

"I wish I knew what he was saying. It seems like he knows me," Sienna said to Tyler.

To which Tyler replied, "He also has the same hourglass that you have. I bet that's him." Tyler was excited to at least find something they had read about in the book.

As they headed towards the newer building, they noticed a friar who had several other friars around him. He looked like the one in charge.

"Buenos dias, Señorita Tico. ¿Cómo estás?" The important-looking man said.

"Good morning, Father. I'm fine. What's going on here?" Sienna said in perfect Spanish.

"We're counting the harvest to report back to Spain," the man said in Spanish, but Sienna heard it in English, unlike when they had first met. There must be some delay or syncing, Sienna thought. "Excuse me, Mrs. Tico, for a second." Another friar came up to the man.

"Father Serra. ¿Cuántos burros tenemos?" the other friar said, to which Father Serra responded, "Twenty-five, Father Jose. Sorry about that, Mrs. Tico. It's a busy time right now.

The fall harvest has just been completed, and we need to prepare a report for Spain. They are always asking us when we will not need any support. If my counts are correct, this will be the first year that we don't need anything from them," Father Serra said as Father Jose jotted down the donkey number and promptly left.

"That's wonderful news. How long will it have been since coming here?"

"Eight long years. God willing, we can continue to have a good harvest. I pray every day for that," Father Serra said as he looked skyward and brought his hands to prayer. "Tell me, Mrs. Tico, how has your study of Costanoan been going? Speaks with Otters was just here. Our translator gathered that he had a warning or something about the river. We could not fully understand it."

"It's coming along, Father. I can understand a few words," Sienna said, knowing full well she had no idea any words in Rumsen, which the Spanish called Costanoan because the tribe lived along the coast.

"That's good. That's good," Father Serra said. "I must get back to the count. Good morning, Mrs. Tico."

"Good morning, Father Serra."

Sienna, Tyler, and Bryant started to walk away, but Father Serra stopped them. "I almost forgot. Our translator made a copy of his Costanoan to Spanish book for you," Father Serra said as he handed Sienna a leather-bound book the size of one of Tyler's chapter books. "I hope this will help you in your studies."

"Thank you, Father. It certainly will."

Sienna turned around and just as she did...

Whoosh!

When they got their eyes focused, the three of them were standing in the small cabin, next to the mirror. This time, Sienna still had the book in her hand.

"Quick. Let's write down everything we learned before we forget," Sienna said as they frantically wrote down all the facts they had gathered from the trip.

Once done, Sienna looked at the Costanoan to Spanish book that made it back with them. "I wonder why this came back with us. I guess I'd better learn some Spanish to make this useful."

CHAPTER SEVEN

PIECES FALL INTO PLACE

The next morning, Sienna, Tyler, and Bryant assessed what they had learned over breakfast.

"Yesterday, we made four trips and explored as much as we could. From what I can calculate, it's the fall of 1779, eight years after Mission Carmel was founded," Sienna said as she read the notebook with their collective notes. "It's clear that the mission has been baptizing natives and they are now living in or near the mission." Sienna was looking down at the notes with her reading glasses on.

"Mom, how are we going to help the sea otters when we can't stay more than a couple of hours?" Bryant said in between eating forkfuls of scrambled eggs.

"It's clear that I have to learn Rumsen and Spanish to communicate with Speaks with Otters. I think once I do that, we can ask him about how to talk with otters. It's clear that there is more than just the mirror," Sienna said as she took a bite of her organic multigrain piece of toast with organic peanut butter and jam.

The four trips to the past had produced a dozen pages of notes. Sienna had used them, along with the two books, to piece together where everything had taken place and what was going on. The Rumsen to Spanish book was confusing since it was handwritten, and Sienna knew neither Spanish nor Rumsen. Well, she knew a little high school Spanish, but that was some twenty years ago.

After breakfast, they hopped in the car and drove to Cannery Row to go back to the library and visit Mrs. Laurie before meeting Jim at the aquarium. Sienna had so many questions for Mrs. Laurie and hoped that she could provide answers.

Mrs. Laurie was in her usual spot along the busy Cannery Row. She did not even lift her head when she said, "Hello, Olivia. How was your trip to the mission?"

"How did you know we went to the mission?" Sienna's eyes were wide, along with Bryant's and Tyler's.

"My dear. I know many things about you. Shall we talk?" Mrs. Laurie said as she rose from her chair and smiled at Sienna. "Come now, I'll put on some tea." Mrs. Laurie turned around and walked toward her 'office.' Sienna, Bryant, and Tyler followed.

"I'm sure you have lots of questions. I hope the book was useful." Mrs. Laurie had placed a fine china teapot on the table and was pouring hot water over the loose-leaf Jasmine tea.

"Yes, very helpful. I figured out that we went back to 1779, Mission Carmel. We met Father Serra and saw Speaks with Otters," Sienna said like she was explaining to a friend how wonderful her recent vacation had been. "I just don't understand why we can do this."

"My dear. It's simple, really. You are related to Olivia. She was one of the original Los Californianos that came over from Spain. Your ancestors traveled all up and down Alta California," Mrs. Laurie said as she blew the steam off of her cup of Jasmine tea.

Sienna pondered that for a second. She had known that her family was from Spain, but they were also from Mexico, Belgium, and Ireland. Her family heritage was a hodgepodge of all sorts of people.

"How can we help the sick sea otters? That's the whole reason I wanted to go back," Tyler said before her mom could say what she was thinking.

"My dear. You can help the sea otters by learning the Rumsen rituals from Speaks with Otters. He is the key to the puzzle. Learn from him and you will find your answer." Mrs. Laurie sat back in her chair and took another sip of her tea. "Now, you must get going. Time is running out!"

Sienna paused for a minute and said, "I have so many other questions. When can we come back?"

"My dear. You have much to do and learn. You will know when to come back." As Mrs. Laurie said that, she got up and said, "My dear. Speaks with Otters is waiting."

It took them a little under five minutes to walk to the aquarium from Mrs. Laurie's to meet Jim for a tour of the artifacts and then off to lunch.

Jim had been out all morning finding more sick sea otters. Two more had been brought into the aquarium.

"Glad to see all of you again. Sorry, I'm such a mess. I just got back from Carmel River Beach." Jim had on high rubber boots caked with mud and sand. "We found two of them high upriver, just about where it starts to turn the bend. Usually, they don't go that high." Jim took off his boots and put on some normal running shoes. "Come into my office and I'll show you the artifacts we have collected."

They all walked through a door into Jim's office, which had a view of the Monterey Bay. Along one wall was a display case filled with artifacts from all over the world. The shelf at eye level had the Rumsen artifacts on it. Jim led them over to that shelf.

"These are the artifacts we have found over the years along the Carmel River. The archeologists say that they are from the late 1700s. Somewhere between 1770-1800."

"That's right around the time the mission first started," Tyler piped up.

"That's right, Tyler. Very good," Jim said as he smiled at her. "We know that because we found some church artifacts along with the Rumsen ones. This one, in particular, is well preserved."

Jim reached over and picked up what looked like a bell. It was tarnished but had the main bell sharp and a handle on top made out of some sort of metal. "This looks like a bell, but it does not have the knocker." Jim turned the bell over and showed them the inside. "See, right there. It's a hole. The archeologists told us that the knocker would be secured there." Jim put the bell back in its place and went through the rest

There were some coins, beads, a clay pot, what looked like metal acorns, a clay plate, and one more thing.

"This is a unique piece right here." Jim held up a goblet. "This is a Communion goblet from the mission. We know because it has an inscription on the bottom." Jim turned it over. Under the rim of the base, an inscription said, 'Safe Travels, Father Serra.'

"That's how we know it's from the mission. This was Father Serra's Communion goblet that he brought from Spain. We know that because there is a picture of it at the mission. I just found this last week. We're in the process of granting it to them." Jim put the goblet back on the shelf.

"We also got the blood test results back. It looks like the otters had mercury in their blood. That points to the biotech companies. One of them, PrimeVac, makes vaccines. They use mercury to preserve them. Actually, it's a special version called thimerosal. They are going to do more tests to see for sure. PrimeVac denies it, of course," Jim said as he rolled his eyes. "The Feds will be coming tomorrow to check it out. Looks like they will shut them down," Jim said as he got his coat on. "Let's go eat," Jim said as he walked back to his desk to find his wallet.

Sienna picked up the bell and looked it over. It had some etchings in the metal, but they were faded. Still, they looked like acorns and sea otters. She flicked her finger at it and heard a dull 'bing.' She then picked up the goblet. It was ordinary looking, with some etchings in it that were faded. The inscription underneath was the only thing that was clear.

"Ready to go?" Jim asked after finding his wallet.

"Yes. We are."

CHAPTER EIGHT

Madness

L unch was at Crystal Fish since they all liked it so much. During lunch, Jim got a text message about another otter. He had to excuse himself to leave early after secretly picking up the check.

The rest of the day was spent at the Dennis the Menace playground. They needed a break from all this traveling back and forth to the past.

After an early dinner at Johnny Rockets, they went back to the cabin.

The artifacts in Jim's office were intriguing. Sienna had found some other books at the cabin that talked about the natives and the Spanish missionaries. There was even a drawing of Father Serra with a Communion goblet that looked like the one Jim had.

They had decided to go back to the past to do some more searching. Now that they knew about the bell and goblet, they would look for them, as well as trying to communicate with Speaks with Otters.

Whoosh!

They were back at the mission in the exact same place as before. This time, they went off towards where they had seen Speaks with Otters.

Sienna had done some studying of the Costanoan to Spanish book with help from Google Translate. She had also brought the book with her.

"Greetings, wise Speaks with Otters," Sienna said as they came upon Speaks with Otters in the same place they had seen him before.

"Hello, Olivia, Juana, and Jose," Speaks with Otters said to them. "Shall we talk more at the village?"

Sienna nodded and followed him to his hut, which was adjacent to the mission. Once inside, they sat down around an altar that was decorated with carvings of acorns and sea otters. On top of it were the bell and mirror.

"I'm glad you came. The otters are in danger," Speaks with Otters said to Sienna in perfect English.

Perplexed, Sienna said, "How can I understand you?"

"When we are close to the bell, mirror, and hourglass, we can communicate. You and I are special in that way. We're part of the same tribe."

"Tribe? What tribe is that?"

"Our ancestors walked out of Africa long ago. We were one tribe then. Our people split off and went two ways. One set, your set, journeyed west into what is now Europe. My set traveled east and walked across a land bridge into what is now Alaska. We walked south until we came here. We have been here ever since." Speaks with Otters paused and looked into Sienna's eyes. She could tell that he was serious. She felt a connection to him. Tyler and Bryant felt the same way like they had met him before.

Tyler broke the silence. "Why do the natives look so sad?"

"The holy men from Spain mean well. They think we are neophytes in the ways of the world. Savages. They see how we live and feel they have to help us. We don't need help. We just have a different way of living." Speaks with Otters paused again. He looked up and then looked at Tyler. "They are sad because our way of life has been taken from us. The holy men want to convert us to worship one God. They call him Jesus, the son of God." He paused again and stroked his beard as if thinking about what to say next. "They are many. We are few, so we decided to do as they say. We have no choice."

Tyler's eyes were wide. She could feel the sense of unfairness well up in her small body.

"That's not fair at all!" Tyler yelled. Speaks with Otters raised his hand like he was stopping the sound from hitting him.

"I know it isn't. But what is done is done. We now have to be at peace with it. Enough about this. We need to discuss the otters."

Speaks with Otters then describes to them what he had observed. The otters told him that the water was bad and that it made them sick. He described the same symptoms that Jim had described to them.

"They tell me it's coming from upstream. Something about madmen. It's hard to understand. They are so sick that it's hard for them to talk."

Madmen, Sienna thought. What madmen? She had seen no madmen anywhere.

"How long have they been sick?"

"Not long. Within the last full moon."

That's strange, Sienna thought. That's the same amount of time the sea otters in the future have been sick.

Just as the thought passed in her mind, there was a commotion outside the tent, yelling in both Spanish and Rumsen. Speaks with Otters jumped up and made his way to the entrance. Sienna, Tyler, and Bryant followed.

A group of five men had ridden into the mission. One of them was slumped over on his horse. Along with their horses, they had several burros with crates slung on either side. One burro, instead of crates, had barrels covered in iron.

"Father. We need your help. Our friend is sick. Is there a doctor here?" the lead man said in a high-pitched squeal like his throat had something stuck in it. He wore a top hat, had brown, beady eyes, and a scruffy beard with light brown dust stuck to it. He was out of place in a mission, let alone on a horse.

The man slumped over the horse was talking incoherently and laughing. He would frantically wave his hands around his face like he was swatting a fly, yet there were no flies.

"Father Jose. Please help the man off the horse and take him to the infirmary. Also, go fetch Old Gabriel. He might be able to help," Father Serra said. He turned to the lead man and said, "How did this man get sick?"

"I'm not sure, Father. He started to get sick a couple of days ago. We are heading to Yerba Buena," the top hat man said. "We're hatters and tailors looking to set up shop there." By this point, the top hat man had dismounted his horse and was standing in front of Father Serra.

"I see. You are welcome to stay until your friend gets better," Father Serra said as he turned to another Father. "Father Juan. Please guide Mister..." Father Serra turned around and looked at the top hat man.

"Mr. Smith," the top hat man said. "John Smith."

"...Mr. Smith and his friends to our guest house." Father Serra turned back to John and said, "We have a stable for the horses near the guest house that will have plenty of water and oats for them. I shall come by once you are settled in and check on how your friend is doing."

"Much obliged, Father," John said as he tipped his hat and took the reins of his horse and followed Father Juan.

Speaks with Otters had a blank stare in his eyes like he had seen a ghost. He walked over to Father Serra and said something that Sienna could not understand. He then walked past them and back into his hut. Sienna and company followed.

As they entered the hut, they saw him with crossed legs in front of the altar, chanting something in Rumsen, as he rocked back and forth. He then opened his eyes and turned to them.

"I have seen that man before. In a vision. It was unclear to me why," Speaks with Otters said. "We must find out where the man got sick."

Whoosh!

They made several trips to the past that night and gathered that the men were from England. Mr. Smith was a hatter, which meant he made hats, while another, Mr. Taylor, was a tailor, and Mr. Cobb made shoes. The other two, the sick one, Mr. Johnson, was a laborer, and Mr. Evans was a chemist who made, of all things, mirrors. The funny thing about all of them was that they all had the same high-pitched voice as Mr. Smith and the shakes. At times, Mr. Evans had to hug himself to stop them.

Sienna thought that on their next trip they would have Speaks with Otters show them the sea otter speaking ceremony. Maybe that would shed some light on the problems with the sea otters in the present.

Sienna felt drained. Every time they went back, she felt more tired. It felt like each trip took another piece of energy, which she would often ask Tyler and Bryant when they were moody. Taking another trip to the past would have to wait until tomorrow. After dinner, Jim texted Sienna about meeting up in the morning. He had good news he wanted to share.

CHAPTER NINE

"**S**ienna, Tyler, Bryant. Great to see you," Jim said. This was the first time they had seen him so happy since they had met not three days ago. "I have some wonderful news." Jim could hardly contain himself. "Shall we go inside and eat?"

Jim had picked First Awakening since it was close to the aquarium and had plenty of seating.

"We found out why the otters were getting sick," Jim said as he put his coffee down. "The Feds were secretly monitoring PrimeVac, even before the otters got sick. They caught them dumping old vaccines down the drain. This morning, they shut the whole place down." Jim had a big smile on his face. "We're going to start to release the otters that are recovered this afternoon."

"That's great! I'm so glad the sea otters won't get sick anymore," Tyler said in between bites of her Belgian waffle with chocolate chips and whipped cream — a rare treat for her.

"Yes. Great indeed. Won't it take time for the old vaccines to wash downriver?" Sienna said.

"No. That's the great thing. The Feds have been filtering the water runoff from PrimeVac for the last couple of weeks. Any old vaccines have either been filtered or already washed to the ocean," Jim said while he waved to the hostess for more coffee. "How about we celebrate? Tonight. Dinner's on me."

"Sure. We can do that," Sienna said as she digested all that Jim had told her. I guess we don't need to go to the past, after all, was her second thought.

"Great. I'll text you later as to the place." Jim's phone rang and he looked down. "Sorry. I need to take this." Jim excused himself and walked outside.

"Mom. Does this mean we won't go back to the past anymore?" asked Tyler.

Sienna had been thinking that as well. Before Sienna could respond, Jim came back in.

"Sorry about that. That was the Feds. They want to take some samples of otter blood. I guess it's the protocol or something like that. I have to get back to meet them," Jim said.

"Are they sure that PrimeVac is the source?" Sienna asked.

"Yup. They caught them red-handed. They even have an insider who tipped them off. I'm so glad this is over."

"Really? An insider. That's good."

"Yup. We can start letting the otters go and get back to normal."

Sienna could not shake the thought about PrimeVac being the culprit. She had done some research, and it turned out that PrimeVac was owned by ProBio. The CEO of PrimeVac, Carlos Montego, was a standup guy. She found it hard to believe that he would allow anyone to dump old vaccines into the river. The only thing she could think of was someone at the company did it behind his back. Either way, she trusted that the Feds had the proof.

"I have to get going. I'm sorry to cut this short but I have to go. I'll text you later about the place for dinner. It's time to celebrate!" Jim said as he gave Sienna a brief hug and then rushed off.

After finishing breakfast, Sienna, Tyler, and Bryant went to the Dennis the Menace playground to relax and enjoy the sunshine. It had been a fast-paced couple of days since they had arrived, and they had hardly had any fun.

As Tyler and Bryant played sea monster, Sienna thought about what Mrs. Laurie had said. She could not get it out of her head that Speaks with Otters held the answer to all of this. As she thought about it, she convinced herself that it did not matter now. The Feds had found the source of sea otter illness. They did not have to go back to the past anymore.

"Tyler. Bryant. Time to go," Sienna said.

"Mom. Really? Let's stay. Where else do we have to go?" Tyler said as she caught her breath.

"It's been two hours! We need to eat."

"Alright. Can we go to Johnny Rockets this time for a burger? Please? Please? Please?"

"Yes. Burgers. Let's get burgers," Bryant said.

"As long as we also eat a salad with the burger," Sienna said.

With that, they hopped in the car for the short drive to Cannery Row and lunch.

After lunch, they strolled along the Row, window shopping, and enjoying the fresh air. Along the way, they took a detour to walk along McAbee Beach. As they walked, they saw a familiar hat.

"Olivia, how was Speaks with Otters?" Mrs. Laurie said as they approached.

"Fine, I guess. We started to talk about the ritual and were interrupted by a group of men. One was sick."

"I see. When are you going back?"

"We're not. They found who was poisoning the sea otters. It was PrimeVac. The Feds caught them dumping vaccines into the Carmel River. They shut them down. They're going to release the sea otters this afternoon."

"I see. I see," Mrs. Laurie said as she paused to look up. "Let's hope that's it." Mrs. Laurie smiled, and her smile revealed her perfectly white teeth. She then put her head down.

"Do you know something I don't?"

Mrs. Laurie looked up again. "Olivia, my dear. I only know what I see." She looked back down and continued to read her book.

Sienna looked perplexed. She was about to say something and then thought better of it.

As they continued their stroll, Jim texted her that they had released a dozen otters and would do more tomorrow. He also sent along with the time and place for dinner. It was just enough time to head over to Carmel-by-the-Sea for a change of pace and some window-shopping before dinner.

CHAPTER TEN

REST AND RELAXATION INTERRUPTED

D inner with Jim was a lavish event. He was so happy that they figured out what was making the sea otters sick. It was such a relief, he said because he was worried about where they would keep them. He was happy that it all worked out in the end.

Sienna, Tyler, and Bryant were also happy it worked out. Now they could enjoy the rest of their vacation without having to worry about the sea otters or take any more trips to the past.

The next day, they all went to Carmel River Beach, which had been reopened to the public. It was so relaxing to just sit on the beach and read a book. Tyler and Bryant loved it as well as they chased each other in the surf.

As they sat down to each lunch, they heard a choir of sirens getting closer.

"Mom, are those sirens?" Bryant said in between bites of his ham and cheese sandwich.

"It sounds like it."

"They are getting closer."

They all turned their heads towards the parking lot and saw a dozen police cars, sirens, and lights flashing, along with a truck from Monterey Bay Aquarium. As the cars parked, one of the officers walked over to the truck as a man was getting out. It was Jim.

"Look, Mom. It's Jim," Tyler said.

"Yes, it is. I wonder what's going on."

Jim and the officer chatted briefly while another man got out of the passenger side of Jim's truck. He opened the tailgate and started to pull out a cage, while Jim gathered up what looked like shields and nets.

"Come on. Let's go see what's going on," Sienna said. All three of them walked up towards the parking lot.

"Jim. What's going on?" Sienna said.

"Someone found a sick otter!" Jim said as he sighed. "We're not sure if it's one we released or not. I'm not getting a ping on my tracker." Jim held up a bulky yellow plastic device with a crude, black and white screen on it. "See. No pings." He showed the screen to Sienna who just shrugged her shoulders.

"Mom. What's going on?" Tyler said

"They found a sick sea otter. Jim's not sure if it's one they released."

"Oh no! I hope it's going to be okay."

"We'll see. I need to get going. I'll text you later," Jim said as he gathered up his shield and net while the other man brought the cage.

As they looked on, they could just see the top of Jim's head as he gently moved the sea otter into the cage.

"Mom. Are they going to be okay?" Tyler said.

"I'm not sure honey. Let's get back to the beach and finish lunch."

They walked back to their spot, finished lunch, and decided to head back to the cabin.

As they twisted and turned along the Carmel Valley, Sienna knew what they had to do.

"Do each of you remember what you're supposed to do?" Sienna said as they gathered in the small cabin.

"Yes. I'm supposed to go to where the sick man is and learn as much as I can about where they were," Bryant said.

"Good. Tyler?"

"I'm going to help you learn the ritual to talk to the sea otters."

"Good. Bryant. You'll need to check in every thirty minutes. You'll then tell us what you know." Sienna could think of no other way than to split up, and since Bryant was older and a boy, the men would not mind him as much. "For this first time, just go to the infirmary and then back since I'm not sure what will happen."

It was true. Sienna had no idea what would happen if they split up, let alone if time ran out. She was reluctant to send Bryant, but she could see no other choice.

Whoosh!

"I see you came back to learn our ways," Speaks with Otters said as he led them into his tent. "The otters will be pleased."

"How do I speak to them? I must find out what is making them sick," Sienna said.

"The ritual is complex, and you need a few things."

"Like what?"

"The hourglass, for one, and the mirror. You'll also need this bell to call them." Speaks with Otters picked up the bell that was on the altar and rang it. The bell sang its siren song of a sweet melody of the nicest sound you ever heard. "You must ring the bell while the mirror is reflecting the light onto the sea. You also must have the hourglass with you."

Speaks with Otters put the bell down.

"When they come, you turn over the hourglass. That's how much time you have to speak with them. No more. No less. You can only call them once a day when the sun is the brightest."

"Is that all there is to it?"

Speaks with Otters smiled, revealing his pearly white teeth. "Olivia. That is the easy part. The hard part is finding where to reflect the sunlight too. It must be where the sea meets the river and is the clearest. That changes daily. There are some days that they don't come because of that."

Sienna pondered that for a minute. Where the sea meets the river. Hmmm. I know where that is but it's always murky and at beach level, impossible to see anything.

As Speaks with Otters continued to go over the ritual, Bryant came back from the infirmary.

"Mom—" Bryant said, out of breath like he had run the whole way. "They..." Bryant leaned over to catch his breath "found...a...mine."

"A mine! What kind of mine?"

"I'm...not...sure."

"Slow down. Slow down. Catch your breath."

Once Bryant had calmed down and caught his breath, he told them that the men were talking about when they could go back to the mine to get more magical metal.

"The sick man, Mr. Johnson, is feeling better. As soon as he can ride, they are going back," Bryant said. "Mom, we need to follow them. Maybe that's what is making the otters sick."

"Did they say what the magical metal was?"

"No. I only heard—"

Whoosh!

They were back in the small cabin.

"Mom. We have to go back," Tyler said.

"Hold on. Hold on. Bryant, did they say which way the magical metal mine was?"

Bryant thought to himself for a minute and said, "Mr. Smith said it was up the Carmel River. It's one of the streams that feeds it to the south. That's all he said." Bryant looked disappointed that he did not remember more.

"That's okay. Before we go back, let's look on Google Maps to see where it could be."

They left the small cabin to go to the big cabin, where Sienna opened her laptop to find a Google Map of the Carmel River valley.

The topology of the valley had not changed. Of course, there were more towns and roads, but the creeks, peaks, and valleys were all still there.

Looking up the Carmel Valley River, there were several smaller, feeder streams and creeks that connected to it — like the veins in a leaf. The first major one was the Las Garzas Creek, then a smaller creek along Southbank Road. Tularcitos Creek was next. It continued along East Carmel Valley Road while the Carmel River went south along San Clemente Road toward an unnamed what looked like a lake. Feeding into this lake was the Carmel River to the south and the San Clemente Creek to the west. The cabin where they were staying was off San Clemente Creek on Dormody Road.

From what Sienna could gather from what Bryant said, the men had gone up the Carmel Valley and then headed south. She had gathered that the magical metal was probably mercury since that's what the mirror was made of, and Speaks with Otters had also mentioned something like that.

She Googled "mercury mines in Carmel Valley" and came across a website called thediggings.com, which had a map and list of claims from all over the world. She zoomed in on the Carmel Valley.

"Bryant. Tyler. Look at this," Sienna said as she pointed to the map. "There are two mines near where we are. One looks like Mercury the other, an Unnamed Prospect. Whatever that means."

"Mom. Both are right off Dormody Road. Not far from here," Bryant said.

"Let's go see if we can find them," Tyler said.

"I don't know. Mercury is poisonous and dangerous."

"Let's just drive by. We don't have to get out of the car," Bryant said.

Sienna thought about that for a second and said, "Okay. No getting out of the car."

They all piled into the Subaru and set off. They did not have to drive long.

As far as Sienna could tell, the first mine was to the west on Dormody Road, while the second was east. From the road, they were hard to see.

"According to the GPS, it should be right over there, along the river," Sienna said as she pointed across the road to the spot.

"I don't see anything. What's a mine supposed to look like?" Tyler asked.

"The only thing I could find describing it was that the soil around the mine looks a different color. There should also be a hole or a marker of some sort with the claim number."

Bryant ran across the street and started to look around.

"Bryant! Come back here," Sienna screamed across the road as she grabbed Tyler's hand and ran after him. "It's dangerous!" Sienna's appeal fell on deaf ears. Bryant had already gone into the brush. As Sienna approached, she could hear the San Clemente Creek.

Splash. Splash. "Mom. I see something," Bryant said as he made his way across the creek.

"Bryant Julio Moraga Valdez Tico Vantalos, stop this instant," Sienna screamed.

"You're in trouble now, Bry," Tyler said, still being dragged by the hand.

"Mom. I see it. I see it." Bryant had made it over to the other side.

On the opposite side of the bank, hidden by a scrub, was what looked like a highway mile marker. It was reflective and in big black letters had M055548 written on it.

Splash. Splash. "Bryant..." Sienna said, trying to catch her breath. "Don't ever do that again. These mines are dangerous. Stay back."

"Mom. See. It's a mine." Bryant pointed to the sign again.

"M055548. That must be the claim number or something like that," Sienna said.

They looked around the sign and saw what looked like a hole with a pile of rocks around it.

"I bet this is where the men in the past came. Where else could they go?" Tyler said.

"There is one more mine east of here. They could have gone there," Sienna said. "Now that we know it's here, let's get going. Don't touch anything."

They made their way across the creek and back to the car. They then drove east along Dormody Road for less than a quarter of a mile and stopped where the next mine would be. The marker was easier to find this time and said MO55548, just like the other one.

Just as they were getting back in the car, Sienna got a text from Jim.

"Jim wants to meet us for dinner. He's sorry he had to rush off. They found more sick sea otters," Sienna said out loud to Tyler and Bryant

CHAPTER ELEVEN

Now What?

"We found three more sick otters today," Jim said as he was eating his pork loin. "I fear we're going to find more. It just makes no sense."

"Were they the same otters or different?" Tyler asked.

"Two were the same. One was different. The weird thing is that the blood tests came back from the Feds. You know, the ones they took a couple of days ago. The otters we released not only had mercury in their blood but also arsenic. To top it all off, the level of mercury, with this more accurate test, was normal for the area. There is always some background mercury in the water. I guess they read the numbers wrong at our local lab." Jim sounded frustrated. "Vaccines never had arsenic in them. Where is that coming from? We're back at square one."

Jim looked tired. His eyelids were heavy, and his face was sunburned from being outside all day. His hair was also a mess.

Sienna could think of nothing to say. She did not want to tell Jim about the trips to the past or Mrs. Laurie. She did not know him well enough for that. She had nothing really to offer. She had no idea either.

"Enough about my day. How was your day?" Jim cracked a smile as best he could.

"It was so fun. We found two mines," Tyler chimed in.

"Really? Where?"

"Near where we're staying. They are old and abandoned. They were mercury mines," Tyler said.

"Mercury mines? I knew that they had gold mines around here, but not mercury." Jim rubbed the bridge of his nose.

"Yes. Bryant found them," Tyler said as Bryant looked up.

"Mom found them on the Internet and we just went there," Bryant said and then went back to his burger.

"Be careful around those old mines. They are unstable," Jim said.

"We will be. Thanks," Sienna said.

Sienna asked Jim if, after dinner, they could go back to his office and look at the artifacts again. He agreed.

When they arrived, Jim excused himself to go check on the sea otters. As Jim left, Sienna picked up the bell. It was the same one that Speaks with Otters had rung in the past. Quickly, she put it in her purse.

"Mom. What are you doing?" Bryant whispered.

"We need this. It's the bell that Speaks with Otters used to summon the sea otters. That's the only way they will come," Sienna whispered back.

"What if he finds out?" Bryant whispered.

"I don't think he'll even know it's gone."

The rest of the evening was spent strolling down Cannery Row. Jim looked more relaxed than at dinner, but he still looked tired. He quickly excused himself, and Sienna, Tyler, and Bryant kept walking.

As they approached Mrs. Laurie's, they could see her outside, reading a book.

"Olivia. Did you get the bell?" Mrs. Laurie said. She was wearing the same wide-brimmed sun hat even though it was approaching twilight.

"Yes. I have it with me."

"Good. Come with me." Mrs. Laurie stood up and led them into her familiar office. Before she sat down, she went over to a small antique hutch to retrieve something.

"Olivia. I have been keeping this for many years," Mrs. Laurie said as she opened her hand.

At first, it was hard to see, but as she moved her hand closer, the object came into focus.

The shiny ball was perfectly smooth. It had a hole through the center of it. Along with the ball, Mrs. Laurie had some metal wire.

"This will make the bell ring to bring the sea otters. It's important that you wrap the ball six times with the wire and then tie it inside the bell. Give it to me and I'll show you."

Sienna reached in her bag and pulled out the bell and handed it to Mrs. Laurie. She took it, flipped it upside down, and showed Sienna.

"See that loop inside the top? That's where you attach it. Make sure to have enough wire to have the sphere go mid-way down. That's important for the correct sound."

"Can you do it for me?" Sienna said.

"No, my dear. My hands are too frail and my eyesight is not what it used to be," Mrs. Laurie said as she handed back the bell and the sphere with the wire. "Now go. You have much work to do."

They left the way they had come in and headed back to the car for the drive back to the cabin.

The whole way, Sienna was going through the sea otter speaking ritual in her head. She just knew that the key to this whole mystery was to talk to the sea otters. They would know why they were getting sick.

After Tyler and Bryant went to bed, Sienna made a solo trip to the past. She needed to know some things and it was best that she went alone. She was proud of Tyler and Bryant for how brave they had been, but it was now up to her to figure out the last piece of the puzzle. It was just too dangerous for Tyler and Bryant to be around when she went back this final time before trying to speak to the sea otters.

CHAPTER TWELVE

RETURN TO THE PAST

The next morning at breakfast, Sienna told Tyler and Bryant that they had to go back to the past and watch *Speaks with Otters* summon the sea otters.

From all the traveling, Sienna had figured out how to extend her stay in the past. It was tricky to pull off, and that's why she needed their help.

"When we get back to the past, we need to quickly go to Speaks with Otters. If I wear his hourglass, we can use them together." Sienna then explained how she had figured this out. "The important thing to remember is that before one runs out, we need to turn the other one. If we do that, we can stay as long as we want. I need both of you to watch the hourglasses to make sure."

Whoosh! They were back in the past.

"We must walk to the bluff, overlooking the beach where the river and ocean meet." Speaks with Otters was already gathering up his supplies. "We must make it before the high sun."

Sienna had originally thought that when they traveled back to the past, it was the same day, over and over again. That turned out to not be true.

When they traveled back, they ended up arriving at the same time, in the morning, but it was always a different day. From what she could figure, the days were roughly the same day as the present, just in 1779. She did not know why they always arrived at the same time.

The hike to the beach was quick since they followed the Carmel River. Once there, they found a mound on the south side of the river. It did not look natural.

"Many moons ago, my ancestors built this mound," Speaks with Otters said. "It allows us to see the best spot. Before the mound, we would build a human pyramid." Speaks with Otters smiled, his perfectly white teeth glistening in the sun. "It is almost time. Quick, let's get to the top."

They all climbed up the mound and could now see where the river and the ocean met. The brown silt swirled in the current as it dumped out of the river.

Speaks with Otters pointed to a deep green patch, just beyond the swirling silt.

"You see there. It's deep blue-green. That's where we aim the mirror. It changes with how much silt is in the river," he said as he pointed to the sea and then the river.

The sun was high in the sky when Speaks with Otters pulled out the mirror and the bell. He positioned the mirror to reflect the sun into the deep blue-green patch as he rang the bell.

It must have taken a good five minutes for a sea otter to appear.

"Otter of the sea. I wish to speak to you," he shouted to the sea otter that appeared.

"You may speak," said the otter. "What is your question?"

"Do you know why the water is poisoned?"

"It is the madness that is doing it. Somewhere upstream. We don't go past the fork. It's too dangerous," said the otter as clearly as they had heard it in the lab.

The sun went behind a cloud, the light disappeared, and so did the sea otter.

"Upstream. Beyond the fork," Sienna said out loud to no one in particular.

Whoosh!

"Mom. We forgot to tip over the hourglass," Tyler said.

"It's okay, honey. We got what we needed. Tomorrow, we need to go to the same place in present time and call the sea otters like Speaks with Otters did," Sienna said as she wrote down all she had learned in their notebook.

✳ ✳ ✳

The next day, after breakfast, they packed up and headed to the same spot *Speaks with Otters* had taken them. This time, they did not find a mound.

"Mom. How are we going to see anything? The mound is gone," Tyler said.

"You'll have to get on my shoulders, Tyler. That's the only way we can get high enough." Sienna had brought the mirror and the bell, with the sphere affixed like Mrs. Laurie had instructed. "We have some time. Let's practice before the sun is at its peak."

For the next hour, Tyler would climb up on Sienna's shoulders as Bryant steadied her. He would then give her the mirror. Tyler would then practice shining it. It was hard to find the same deep blue-green spot they had seen in the past. To make matters worse, the rains over the last weeks had swollen the river to its peak. The silt field was also much bigger and the winds were picking up. The weather report called for a chance of rain in the afternoon, as the clouds moving in from the north were dark with rain.

"It's almost time. Let's practice one more time," Sienna said as Tyler climbed up on Sienna. As she reached for the mirror, a gust of wind made Bryant slip and the mirror fell out of his hand, landing on the ground with a crash.

"Oh no! The mirror!" Tyler said as Bryant got up and looked down. The mirror had landed flat on the ground and cracked like a spider web. Bryant reached down, but Sienna quickly put Tyler down and stopped him.

"Watch out. It might come apart if we pick it up. Let me look."

Sienna bent down to assess the damage. The mirror had what looked like a thousand cracks in it. When she picked it up, the frame held the fragments in place.

"Whew! It looks like it's intact. I'm not sure how well it's going to reflect."

"Mom. The sun! It's at its height. We need to hurry. The clouds are starting to come in as well," Tyler said.

"Quick. Tyler. Get on my shoulders. Bryant. Be careful with the mirror. Ready? Let's do this."

Tyler climbed up onto Sienna's shoulders. Bryant gently gave her the mirror. This time, it was a lot harder to get a reflection, and the spot was a lot smaller than before.

The spot they had practiced was not covered in silt due to the winds kicking it up. The new spot was much farther out and harder for the mirror to reflect to.

"Tyler. We must hurry. Hold it still. Bryant, ring the bell."

Ring. Ring. Ring. Bryant rang the bell. Nothing happened.

"Ring it again. Tyler, hold the mirror still."

Bryant rang the bell again. Sienna strained to hold Tyler still as she reflected the sunlight to the spot. The wind was picking up and the clouds were moving in.

"Keep ringing it," Tyler said as she balanced on her mother.

After what felt like forever, a small head popped out of the water. It was a sea otter.

"Mom. Look. It's River," Tyler said, pointing to the light. "Hi, River. We want to ask you a question."

"Go ahead," River said.

"What is making you and your friends sick?"

"It's the madness. Upstream. We can't go any farther than the fork. The water is bad. Please help us," River said and then a dark cloud blocked the sun. The light and River were gone.

"That's what the sea otter in the past said," Tyler said out loud. "What's the madness?"

"I'm not sure, but we'd better get back to the car. It's about to rain and we don't have any jackets."

Just as they reached the car, the dark clouds overhead opened up and dumped buckets of rain.

Sienna decided to drive to the aquarium to see if Jim was around. She had to somehow convince him to look upstream without telling him about traveling to the past and talking to sea otters.

Jim was in his office when they arrived.

"I'm glad you came by. We're still hunting down the source of the arsenic, but once we get the otters out of the water, they recover quickly," Jim said as he stood up to hug Sienna. Just then, his phone beeped. "Oh. Sorry about this. Give me a sec." He walked out of the room.

Quickly, Sienna took out the bell and replaced it on the shelf. Jim came back a minute later.

"So, what brings you by?"

"We just wanted to see if you had made any progress. Have you looked farther upstream? Above the first fork?"

"We don't think it's coming from the river," Jim said. "Our new theory is that it's from the old semiconductor plant in Watsonville. Apparently, they use arsenic to make computer chips. It was located above the Elkhorn Slough in the late 1970s. They demolished it in the late 1990s but did not take away any of the waste. It's a superfund site so it's been a fight on what to do with it. We think the heavy rains over the last couple of weeks washed it down the slough and into the ocean."

"Oh, I see. But you found the sick sea otters on Carmel River Beach. Doesn't that mean it's upstream from there?" Sienna said.

"Not really. There is an abundance of food right off of Carmel River Beach. My guess is that it's just a coincidence."

This did not sit well with Sienna, but she had no way to tell him that she had traveled to the past and spoken with sea otters.

"We have limited resources to investigate this. The Feds will be going there this afternoon to take measurements."

"What if it's not that?"

"Then I don't know what to do. It's the best lead we have." Jim's voice sounded defeated.

"Okay. I hope it works out. We should get going," Sienna said.

"Oh. Okay. I really appreciate you coming by. Maybe we can get dinner tonight."

"Sorry. Not tonight. We're busy. Maybe tomorrow. I'll text you."

"Um. Okay."

Jim walked them out. As they walked to the car, Tyler said, "Mom, how come you did not tell him?"

"We don't have any proof yet. All we have is the crazy story of speaking with sea otters and traveling to the past. We need something more than that. I'm afraid we won't convince him without something concrete that can convince him."

CHAPTER THIRTEEN

We Need a Sign

Once back at the cabin, Sienna knew what she needed to do.

"Tyler. Bryant. We're going to have to follow the men in the past. That's the only way to figure out if they are responsible in some way for making the sea otters sick."

"How are we going to do that, Mom?" Bryant said.

"We're going to have to follow behind them so that we're not seen. We also need to make sure we get the hourglass from Speaks with Otters so we can stay longer. It's up to us now. We must find what's making the sea otters sick."

Whoosh!

"Wait right here. I'll be back in five minutes," Sienna said as she dropped Tyler and Bryant off at Speaks with Otters' tent. "When I get back, we'll get going."

Sienna had known that Mr. Johnson was feeling better and that the whole crew would be heading off to whatever mine they had found the magical metal in.

The three of them would follow them, at a safe distance, while keeping track of the time with the two hourglasses.

Sienna was back when she promised and just in time to see the five men and their burros heading out of the mission. The burros had the same lead-covered crates, along with more supplies. They moved slowly under the load, which was going to make it easier to keep up with them on foot.

"We need to keep our distance. If they spot us, we need to run. If we get split up, meet at Speaks with Otters' tent." Bryant and Tyler nodded. "Okay. They are just leaving the mission. Let's get going."

The men had started off just before the high sun, which Sienna figured was around noon. As she expected, the over-burdened burros were setting the pace. They could hear their snorts, along with the men coaxing them along.

Sienna had mapped out the most likely route they would take on Google Maps. Her hunch was that they would follow the river east along with the natural flow of the Carmel River to the sea. Based on driving and Google Maps, the elevation gain was not as abrupt. Better still, the Rumsen had been up and down the valley so much that they had worn a trail that was wide enough for horses.

As expected, the group of men headed east toward the main trail, El Camino Real, modern-day Highway 1 or the Cabrillo Highway. They then turned north until they hit the mouth of the valley, then headed east. The river was south of them since that was the Rumsen trail.

"According to the maps I looked at, the fork should be about nine miles up this way. At our pace, we'll get there in three hours." Sienna looked down at the hourglasses. One was completely empty while the other was halfway through. "Remind me to flip the other one when this one gets to a quarter full."

Both Tyler and Bryant nodded.

The hike was going smoothly. The Carmel Valley was a combination of trees and shrubs with the odd meadow. They decided to stay at least a quarter-mile behind, thinking that it was close enough to hear the burros and far enough to run and hide if needed.

"Mom. I'm cold," Tyler said as she hugged herself.

Sienna had felt the chill as well. The clouds were starting to get darker and darker.

"I'm cold too!" Bryant said.

"Tyler, take my shawl. Bryant, you're going to have to make do."

As they walked, the clouds got darker and darker. A light rain was starting to fall. They had been going for about three turns of the hourglass, which was about two and a half hours or so. They should be close to the first fork.

The wind was starting to pick up. The rain was getting heavy. It was now coming down in sheets. The men up ahead started to slow down. The horses and burros were slipping. Sienna could just barely make out that they were at the first fork in the river.

The rain continued. Thunder and lightning lit up the valley. The burros up ahead got spooked and one of the lead cases slipped off and fell into the river. It sank to the bottom as the river swelled rapidly.

"Tyler, Bryant. We need to get to high ground. The river is rising quickly and it could be a flash flood." Sienna grabbed both of them and started to find higher ground.

They slipped and slid down in the mud as they struggled to get away from the river. The rain had let up a bit, but it was still coming down in sheets and was being whipped around by the wind.

"Get on your hands and knees. We need to get to higher ground." The sides of the hill they were climbing were now all mud. The water was rushing down. They struggled and slipped several times but managed to make it up the hill, fifty feet above the river. The men upstream were not so lucky.

"OMG. Mom. It's a wave." Tyler pointed upstream. Both Sienna and Bryant looked. Through the sheets of rain, they could see what looked like a six-foot wave of water. Since they were high up, they could see it coming down the north fork of the river. It was heading right towards the men.

"Tyler. Bryant. Look away." Sienna held both of their heads towards her chest just as the wave swept the men, horses, and burros up. They tumbled head over heels down the river, past where they had just been.

Whoosh!

They were back in the small cabin.

"Mom. What happened to the men?" Tyler was crying. Bryant was shivering. Sienna was in shock.

Sienna put both arms on Tyler's shoulders and looked her in the eye. "Tyler. You're okay. Don't worry about them. We're fine." She turned around and saw Bryant. She moved toward him, pulling a blanket off the bed. "Here. Put this around you." She gathered each of them under a separate arm and held them tight. She did not notice that the two hourglasses around her neck were gone.

After they had taken showers and changed their clothes, they ate dinner. Tyler and Bryant did not say much. Sienna felt they were in shock from the experience. She knew that she was.

After putting both of them to bed, Sienna went to the small cabin and added to the notebook what they had experienced. She also thumbed through the older entries, trying to piece the mystery together.

It was clear to her that the five men were going to some sort of mine. The iron cases that their burros carried were part of that. Sienna had figured that they were important, so she had snuck into where they were stored to take a look.

She had done this the day before as part of her solo journey to the past.

She had tried to lift them, but they were unmovable by just her. Each had a lock. There were no other marks on them.

While she was there, she had found a nail and etched into the metal the letters "OT." She wanted to make sure that if she saw anything like them in the present, they might give her a clue if she could place them with the men.

The other thing she did was to give Jim a clue to believe her and take a look at the first fork. She now knew what was making the sea otters sick and the only way to save them was to convince Jim. She hoped her plan would work. There was only one way to find out.

CHAPTER FOURTEEN

"Jim. I'm so glad you could see us this morning."

"Of course. Always happy to see you."

"Jim, I need to tell you something. It's going to sound crazy but please bear with me." Sienna was hoping Jim would be open-minded.

"Um. Sure."

"The sea otters are getting sick from the Carmel River. You need to send people to look at the first fork," Sienna said matter-of-factly. "If you don't, they will still get sick."

"How do you know this?" Jim looked confused.

"You have to trust me on this. I can't tell you how I know."

"Sienna. This is really odd. I can't just direct people to go searching someplace on a hunch. I'll get fired." Jim was now pacing around his desk and stroking his mustache.

"I figured you might say that. So there is one thing I can tell you that might help prove that it's worth doing."

"What might that be?"

Sienna walked towards the wall of artifacts and grabbed the Father Sierra Communion cup.

"Remember the other day, you showed me this cup and knew that it was Father Sierra's because of the inscription on the bottom." Sienna held the cup out in front of her.

"Yeah. So?"

"Look at the inscription now." Sienna walked over and gave the cup to Jim. He took it and looked at the inscription. His eyes got big. He looked at Sienna and then looked at the bottom of the cup again.

He pulled out his cell phone and started to dial.

"Gary. It's Jim. We need to go to the first fork of the Carmel River. I know. I know. Trust me. Get a team. Full Hazmat."

Jim hung up, looked at Sienna, and then left the room — taking the cup with him.

"Mom. What just happened?" Bryant said.

"Jim got what he needed."

Sienna, Tyler, and Bryant let themselves out of Jim's office.

They walked down Cannery Row towards Mrs. Laurie's. Sienna wanted to confirm one more thing.

Mrs. Laurie was sitting outside with her big sun hat on. As they approached, she said nothing, just got up, and led them into her office.

"Olivia. Nice to see you." Mrs. Laurie lifted her head up to reveal a big smile filled with pearly white teeth."

"It's good to see you again too, Speaks with Otters."

"My dear. How did you know?"

"It's your teeth. Pearly white even back in 1779. Hard to do that back then. How come you did not tell me?"

"Would you have believed me? You were skeptical just like Jim until you had proof."

"True." Sienna reached in her pocket and took out the metal sphere. "This belongs to you. Thanks for all your help."

"My pleasure, my dear."

"Will the sea otters be okay?"

"My dear. I'll find out when you do."

After they left Mrs. Laurie's, they headed down Cannery Row to play some video games. The last six days had not been that fun for any of them. So much for a relaxing vacation.

As they were playing miniature golf at Highway 1 Golf, Sienna got a text from Jim.

Found a lead container full of arsenic at the fork in the river. It was leaking. Hazmat has it fully contained. Thanks, OT. Dinner?

Sienna thought for a minute before texting him back. She was thankful that her hunch on the lead container was correct. She had done some research on arsenic and found that it was often used to make mercury vapor, which was how you made mirrors. The fact that the men all had high-pitched voices and one was sick meant that they were breathing in mercury vapor. Arsenic was critical to making it. Vaporizing the mercury was required to make mirrors. Breathing in the vapor made your voice high-pitched. Too much exposure made you sick. Once Sienna had all the pieces, it made sense to find the arsenic.

Sienna texted back, "Sure. What time?"

"Mom, I have to ask. What did Jim see on the bottom of the cup?"

Sienna was driving north up Highway 1. It was Sunday and the traffic was light. It had been a long week and not as restful as she wanted.

"Well. I needed to put something that would make him believe that I knew what I was talking about." Sienna paused.

"What did you write? C'mon, Mom. Tell me. Please. Please."

"Tyler. Drama free; way to be. Remember?" Sienna said as she smiled and laughed.

"Mom. Geez. You always do this to me."

"Alright. Alright. I wrote crème brûlée and OT."

"I get the crème brûlée, but what's OT?"

"It stands for Olivia Tico. I inscribed OT on each of the cases. I put it in several places in hopes that at least one of the marks would survive. When they pulled the lead box out of the river, I had told Jim to look for OT. That way, he would know I was telling the truth."

"Clever. Very clever, Mom."

"Yes, Tyler. Sometimes moms can be clever." Sienna smiled and turned up the radio as they sped home to San Francisco.

CHAPTER FIFTEEN

FULL CIRCLE

It had been about a month since the last trip to Monterey. Sienna, Tyler, and Bryant were looking forward to seeing Jim and relaxing for the weekend. Instead of Cabin 84, Sienna had booked them into the Monterey Plaza Hotel & Spa. It was Sienna's favorite and at the end of Cannery Row.

Jim had been giving them updates on the sea otters. All of the ones treated at the aquarium had been released and none had come back. It had been three weeks since all of them had been released.

Jim had come up to San Francisco to visit the Academy of Sciences the previous week. He gave a lecture on how the team had figured out how the sea otters were getting sick. The talk and the report said nothing about what Sienna had written on the communion cup or what she had engraved on the lead containers. The only mention was:

Special thanks to SV and family.

"Mom, how come Jim did not thank you by name?" Tyler said as Sienna took Del Monte Blvd. off of Highway 1. "He only said thanks to SV."

"Tyler, it's going to be hard for grownups to believe that we traveled back in time to help Jim with the sea otters. It's just one of those things that's better left unsaid."

"That hardly seems fair, Mom. I mean, we're the ones who solved the mystery. How come we don't get any credit?"

"Tyler, I understand that you're upset about it, but it's really better this way. It's just good that we could help. Sometimes, you have to be okay with that."

Tyler thought about that for a second. "Okay. I still don't like it."

They checked into the Monterey Plaza and decided to relax at the pool until dinner. Jim had made reservations at Crystal Fish but before dinner, Jim wanted them to swing by the aquarium for a surprise. Sienna was not a big fan of surprises, but she figured why yuck someone else's yum?

Sienna also wanted to swing by BookBuyers before visiting the aquarium. She had called ahead and, as luck would have it, they had a book she was looking for.

✳ ✳ ✳

"Here you go. Feel free to look through it before you buy it," the clerk behind the counter said.

"Thanks." Sienna grabbed the book and looked in the index for what she was looking for.

It was an old book. Out of print since 1925 but BookBuyers had recently come across it and Sienna was glad when they called her about it.

The Mystical Adventures of Juan Bautista de Anza in the Carmel Valley was the book that Mrs. Laurie had let her borrow.

Ever since their last trip back to the past, she had always wondered about something and hoped that the book would give her the answers she needed. She was not disappointed when she turned to the right page and read aloud to Tyler and Bryant.

"Smith, who eventually made it to the Presidio in San Francisco, recalls the flash floods of 1779 that swept them downriver. James Smith, 26, recalls that they had clung onto a passing log and were repeatedly struck by lightning. Smith was the only one to survive and, miraculously, their burros and horses survived." Sienna put the book down.

"Mom, were those the men we saw?" Tyler said.

"Yes. Looks like only one person made it after being struck by lightning. I was wondering what happened to them."

Sienna bought the book and then they headed off to the aquarium to meet Jim for whatever surprise he had in store.

"Mom, can we go down Cannery Row?" Bryant said. "I want to stop by Just Sugar."

"Yes. Me too. Me too," Tyler said.

"You guys know the rule. No candy before dinner."

"We know. We know," Tyler and Bryant said in unison as they rolled their eyes.

They made their way down Cannery Row and as they approached Just Sugar, they noticed that Mrs. Laurie's shop was closed up.

"Excuse me, what happened to Mrs. Laurie next door?" Sienna said to the clerk at Just Sugar.

"Oh. She left a couple of weeks ago. Just up and left. No one knows why. No forwarding address. Nothing. It's like she vanished into thin air. What's strange is that she had just moved in. Not even three months ago."

"Really? No one knows where she went? She just up and left?" Sienna said as she massaged her neck.

"Yes. It was so weird. One day, she was outside her office, just like she always was. The next day, her whole office was cleaned out. Like she did it during the night," said the clerk.

"Oh. Okay. Thanks. So strange," Sienna said.

With the candy secured, they made their way to meet Jim, who had VIP passes waiting for them at the entrance.

"Sienna, Tyler, and Bryant, wonderful to see you," Jim said as they entered his office. Jim gave Sienna a big hug and a light kiss on the lips. They had been seeing each other when Jim came up to San Francisco. They had gone out to dinner without Tyler and Bryant and were now talking daily.

"Kissing! Gross" Tyler said as she tugged on the collar of her shirt.

Jim and Sienna laughed.

"I'm so glad you guys could come by before dinner. I have something for each of you." Jim went around to his desk and opened the top drawer. He pulled out a pile of papers and some laminated cards.

"I know that we can't talk about the huge impact all of you have had on saving the otters." Jim had come around his desk and was now standing in front of all three of them. "I wanted to do something special for each of you in recognition of your valuable contributions. So, I wanted to give you these."

Jim handed each of them one of the laminated cards.

"These are lifetime passes to the aquarium. You can come anytime you want. They also allow you to come to our fundraisers and other special functions."

Tyler looked at the shiny card. It had her picture on it and her name. In the upper right-hand corner, there was a gold seal with the letters UPOTO with the words Monterey and Carmel under them.

"What does UPOTO mean?" Tyler said out loud.

"Oh that. That is a special level that I created just for you three. Officially, it's my new research code for the new grant I received. What it really means is Undercover Protector of the Otters. With that sticker, you're now part of the ongoing effort to protect sea otters in Monterey and Carmel," Jim said with a smile.

"How cool!" Tyler's eyes and mouth were wide. Sienna was blushing, and even Bryant was impressed.

"Thanks, Jim. You did not have to do this for us," Sienna said, smiling.

"My pleasure. We would never have found out what was making the otters sick without your help. I just wish I could make what you did more public, but I don't think anyone would understand."

"That's okay," Tyler piped in. "We know, and that's good enough."

TO BE CONTINUED...

CPSIA information can be obtained
at www.ICGtesting.com
Printed in the USA
FSHW022352200621
82544FS

9 781034 384199